LOTS OF LATKES

A special thanks to
Shari Greenspan for all her help.
In memory of my aunt, Irene Cohen,
who made lots and lots of latkes
for my family and showed us lots
and lots of love.
                                    —S.L.

For Esme amd Arne—Thanks.
                                    —V.J.R.

LOTS OF LATKES

Sandy Lanton

illustrated by Vicki Jo Redenbaugh

KAR-BEN
PUBLISHING

Long ago in a faraway village nestled between two tall mountains, lived an old woman named Rivka Leah. One snowy day, a few days before Hanukkah, Rivka sent notes to each of her friends. The notes read:

Come to my house the first night of Hanukkah just before sundown, and we will celebrate the holiday together. Bring your menorah and something good to share with latkes.

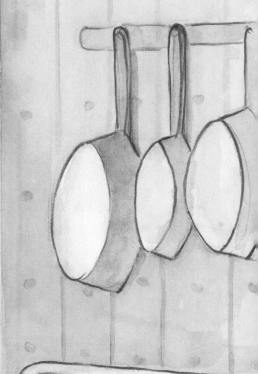

Moshe the milkman read the note and replied: "I would be delighted to attend. I will bring my menorah and I will prepare sour cream to eat with the latkes."

Chana, who tended a fruit orchard, sent her response: "I would love to come, and I will bring my menorah. I have plenty of apples stored in my cellar, so I will make applesauce to go with the latkes."

Avrom the fisherman wrote his answer: "I'll arrive before sundown and I will bring my menorah. I live near the lake, so I will catch some fish to fry."

Manya the baker answered: "I'll be there for sure, and I'll bring my menorah. I put up lots of jars of jelly this fall, so I'll make jelly donuts for dessert."

The morning of the first night of Hanukkah dawned bright and sunny. Moshe went to his barn to get a bucket of cream so he could make sour cream. But the cow knocked over the bucket.

"Now what should I do?" he said to the cow. "I can't go to the party with nothing." He went back to his house to think about what to bring.

Chana went to the cellar to get apples for her
applesauce. But all the apples had rotted. "Now
what should I do?" she said to her cat. "I can't
go to the party empty-handed." She went upstairs
to her kitchen to search her pantry.

Avrom took his fishing pole to the lake. He cut
a big hole in the ice and sat down. But the fish
weren't biting.

"Now what should I do?" he said to his faithful dog. "I can't be the only one to arrive with nothing." He sat for a while longer, whittling a twig and thinking.

Manya went to the pantry
to get some sugar to make
her jelly donuts. But the
mice had eaten all the
sugar.

CORN

POT

SUGAR

"Now what should I do?" she said to the mice. "I can't go to the party without something to share. I can bring some jars of jelly, but is that enough?" She made herself a cup of tea and sat down to think.

That evening, as the guests arrived, Rivka Leah greeted them warmly at the door.

"Happy Hanukkah, friends. I have a fire roaring, and the kettle is on for tea. And of course I made lots of latkes. Did you bring something to share?"

"Of course," boomed Moshe, "but my cow knocked over the cream, so I brought latkes instead."

"And my apples were rotted, so I made latkes, too," said Chana. "The fish weren't biting, so I, too, made latkes," said Avrom.

"The mice ate the sugar, so I also brought latkes, along with some jars of jelly," Manya reported.

"So many latkes!" said Rivka Leah.
She laughed and laughed.
"Lots of latkes!" Chana and Moshe joined in.
"Lots and lots of latkes," Avrom agreed.
Soon all the friends were laughing.

"I am great at telling the story of Hanukkah," said Moshe.
"While I was fishing, I whittled a dreidel," added Avrom.
"And I brought my fiddle to play cheerful music," said Manya.

"I know plenty of Hanukkah songs I can lead," said Chana. "And I made up a Hanukkah dance that I can teach everyone," said Rivka Leah.

Moshe told the story of Hanukkah in his
booming voice, acting out the miracle of
the Maccabee soldiers and the small jar
of oil that lasted for eight nights.

The friends ate, drank, played dreidel, sang and danced by the blazing light of the menorahs until dawn shed its rosy light over the valley.

Rivka Leah's Latke Recipe: (serves 3-4)

4 medium potatoes

1 medium onion

2 tsp. salt

2 eggs

2 Tbsp. flour

1/2 c. oil

Grate potatoes and onion into a bowl. Add salt, eggs and flour, and mix well. Heat oil in pan, and spoon by tablespoonfuls into oil. Fry until brown around the edges, then turn and fry other side. Drain on paper towels.

Serve with sour cream and applesauce.

KAR-BEN PUBLISHING, INC.
A division of Lerner Publishing Group
241 First Avenue North
Minneapolis, Minnesota 55401 U.S.A.
800-4KARBEN

Website address: www.karben.com

Library of Congress Cataloging-in-Publication Data

Lanton, Sandy.
Lots of latkes : a Hanukkah story / by Sandy Lanton ; illustrated by
Vicki Jo Redenbaugh.
p. cm.
Summary: Rivka Leah invites her neighbors to a Hanukkah party, but a
series of mishaps causes each of them to bring the same dish — latkes.
ISBN: 1-58013-091-7 (lib. bdg. : alk. paper)
ISBN: 1-58013-061-5 (pbk. : alk. paper)
[1. Hannukah—Fiction. 2. Jews—Fiction.] I. Redenbaugh, Vicki Jo,
ill. II. Title.
PZ7.L293 Lo 2003
[Fic]—dc21
2002152166

Manufactured in the United States of America
1 2 3 4 5 6 — DP — 08 07 06 05 04 03